Withdrawn

Unknown Author

Unknown Author
based on a true story

Sidney

2006

Unknown Author

It happened three days ago. I remember it vividly. They say your life passes before your eyes when you're about to die, but there was no time for reminiscing. By the time I realized what was happening, it was over. I can still feel it. The muffled sound. The punch in my chest. The burning in my left shoulder blade. I gasped for breath as I looked down to see the damage they had done. My back felt wet. It took only a second for it to register. They'd found me. All the precautions. All the secrecy. A dozen towns. Half as many names. All the bullshit and heartache. All for nothing. In a split second, none of it mattered. They'd found me. The fucking bastards found me.

AUTHOR'S NOTE AND ACKNOWLEDGMENTS

This book is my life. At times I've wished I could forget my past, but then I realize it is my past which has formed my present self. I am thankful for the lessons I have learned and for the life I am living. Although my book describes the trials and heartache of what I've been through, I feel I should point out that there were some positive things along the way. I've seen many beautiful places, and have been shown unbelievable kindness and compassion at times when I thought I would never make it. Words will never be enough to express my gratitude, but please know you will always be in my heart.

I would like to give special thanks to: my families, my friends and first-draft readers (C.A., S.B., S.L.), my friends and editors (K.W., M.B., T.K.), my friends and mentors (G.H., P.C., M.M.), and my friends and supporters (whose names are too numerous to mention)

I would like to give extra special thanks to "Carrie", "Liz" and "Patrick"

I love you all.

UNKNOWN AUTHOR

CHAPTER ONE

UNKNOWN AUTHOR

It's 10 a.m. How quickly things can change without warning. Allen should be opening the studio right now.

Oh, honey, I'm so sorry. I never meant to put you through this. They told me everything would be fine. I was protected. I should have told you. I thought it would only worry you, make you paranoid like me. Maybe I thought you wouldn't want me. I can't think about that now. It doesn't matter anymore. I've totally screwed up your life. I made the choice to do what I did. Granted, I never dreamed it would follow me this far, but it was my choice. I never gave you that luxury. Wake up, baby, you can do this. I'll help you through it. I'm with you.

He should be opening the studio. Our studio. Warming up the computer, greeting customers, making some coffee. Instead, he's burying me today. His new bride. And he has no idea why. Who would want to kill his lovely wife? Why? A sniper, they said. A sniper. The word sounded foreign to his ears. This wasn't some movie, for God's sake. It was his life. What was supposed to be a new beginning. He and Max had agreed, without question, that I was the one.

Even though I'd missed out on the first ten years of his life, Max and I became fast friends. I was so nervous about meeting him. Allen and I had dated for a while, and everything was going well. I could tell how crazy he was about his son, and I didn't know how I'd fit into the whole picture. I guess you could say Max and I bonded right away. He was so excited when Allen asked how he felt about us getting married. Allen was worried about how Max would react, but his fears quickly vanished when Max cheerfully said, "Does this mean Sidney gets to be

3

my stepmom?" Allen knew I would be more than okay with the thought of having Max as a stepson. A parachuting accident had left me with a medical discharge from the Army, a broken pelvis, a damaged uterus, ovaries, and bladder. It also left me unable to have children. He knew how much I loved children, and had no doubt I would be a grateful stepmom.

I'll never forget the day they proposed to me. It started out as a terrible day. I can still picture it. There I was, on my way to school, when something didn't seem quite right. I thought the brake pedal felt mushy under my foot. What a strange sensation. You don't even realize how accustomed you've become to that space between your brake pedal and the floor—until that space is gone. This time, my foot went all the way to the floor. My brakes were gone. I had to downshift my way to a semi-stop at every intersection until I reached my mechanic's shop. They did give me a ride to school, but they also said my car would be in the shop for at least a few days. Great.

I made it to class on time. Barely. Slipping into my seat and trying to forget about my brakes, I was hit with surprise number two. A quiz for which I had obviously missed the announcement. Perfect. It was only nine in the morning and the day was already a stinker. After the quiz that I probably bombed, my mechanic called with the damage. Eight hundred dollars. Where was I going to get eight hundred dollars? I was a starving art student. I hated to do it, but I called Allen to ask if he could pick me up after my last class. I knew it was going to be an inconvenience to say the least. He was a town away, had to take care of customers, pick Max up at day camp, and get back in time for Max's softball game. Of course, he said, "No problem." He was in an especially good mood, but I still didn't suspect a thing. I was too busy stewing over the failed quiz and eight hundred dollar repair bill. Little did I know, he and Max had been out shopping for an engagement ring that day. Allen later told me that Max was so excited about the proposal, that when they stopped to buy some coffee, Max couldn't stand still. When Allen asked him what was wrong, he huffed, "Well, it's a fine time to be buying coffee, Dad."

They caught me completely off guard when they called me to the basement to hear the new song that Max had learned on his keyboard. In reality, Max was providing the background music for what would be his dad's proposal to me. I was shocked. We all laughed and cried and celebrated with some sparkling cider. Then we went to Max's softball game, which they won, and had ice cream cones on the way home.

We were married six months later. Max and I spent a lot of time together when Allen would work late. Sometimes it felt like Max and I were closer than Max and Allen. I know that's not true, but Allen could get a little consumed with work sometimes. Regardless, everything was finally coming together for me. I had a wonderful husband, an incredible stepson, and my life was on its way to being normal for once. We were a family now. At least, until three days ago.

CHAPTER TWO

You have to go pick him up, sweetie. You know how the traffic around Houston gets. Are you sure this is a good idea? Maybe he's too young. Has he ever been to a funeral? What are you planning to tell him? You can't exactly tell him a sniper shot his stepmom through the living room window. Oh, God, I should have told you. I should have left you alone is what I should have done. I had no right to involve you and Max in this. But I dropped my guard. I fell in love. Didn't I deserve to be loved?

It's amazing how death is all I am now. I'm not a person. I'm not a cold breeze that brushes the cheek of my loved ones. What am I to them? A memory? It's a funny concept if you really think about it. I'm an emotion. Despair. A horrible weight pressing down on them, stealing their air. To me, I just am. I can't touch them. I can't tell them what really happened, who did it, why. I can't tell them I'm sorry. I seem to be able to read Allen's thoughts.

I'll wait here, sweetie.

Usually I would jump at the chance to go to the airport and pick up Max. But not today.

I didn't know what to expect from death. I'd thought about it many times since this all began. Imagining your own death isn't something a nineteen year old normally has to deal with, but my situation was anything but normal. Now, at age thirty-five, I know. There's no bright light, no pearly gates. Just a change. One minute they see you, the next they don't. Abracadabra. Alacazaam. Your body's there, of course, but not you. Your body's not you.

Max.

Hey, kiddo, don't look that way.

This isn't fair. He doesn't deserve this; he's just a kid. The happiest kid I've ever known. Now look what I've done. He shouldn't have to be dealing with this.

I'm still here, sweetie. I haven't left you. Oh, my God, I guess I have. In your eyes I have. I wish I could tell you how much you mean to me. You gave me a reason to try, kiddo. I know you'll never understand this, but you were worth it.

CHAPTER THREE

(My Funeral)

It's so strange, watching your own funeral. You're like an outsider, even though it's all because of you. You see friends you care about, but never seemed to have enough time to visit. Now here they are, paying one last visit to me. You realize that little things are so insignificant, like who still has your favorite book, or whose turn is it to buy lunch. It's just stuff. And money? Money just buys more stuff. None of it matters now. It's hard to describe, but it feels good seeing all the people I love in one place together. Why don't people do this when they're alive? Why don't we have living "funerals" to celebrate one's life before we find ourselves mourning their death? Everyone's so sad because they miss me; they can't see me. But it's hard for me to feel the same sadness when I'm right here. If they could only know I'm right here. It feels good to see everyone. Who am I fooling? This doesn't feel good at all. It feels awful. Look what everyone is going through because of me. I should have stayed to myself. I knew better than to make friends.

Wow, it's a beautiful day, though. There's a little bit of a crisp in the air, and the leaves are changing. I guess everything changes in its time. Nothing can ever stay the same. The Impressionists knew it. They tried to capture those fleeting moments, that perfect light. Today would have been an ideal day to paint. Autumn has always been my favorite time of year.

Mark is here. How awkward is this? Maybe Allen won't notice him. Pretty hard not to notice, though. Mark has always looked the part—perfectly pressed suit, dark glasses, no smile. Allen sees him. I can tell he recognizes him, but he's not quite sure from where.

SIDNEY

Yes, sweetie, you've seen him before. The day I died, out in the park.

Our house sits on the edge of a park which I've always loved, but have equally feared. The scenery is great, but secluded enough to make me feel vulnerable. Seclusion is a funny thing to someone like me. There's a fine line between seclusion and isolation. Allen never understood why I freaked out when he'd left the curtains open, and especially when he'd left the doors unlocked. How nice it must be to live without fear. I can't remember a time like that for me. I guess a lot of things I did will make more sense to him now.

There had been so many officers that day, so many questions; the shock of it all. But now it's clear. During the investigation of the park, Mark stood out from the rest. Just like now at my funeral. He's looking at Allen, nodding. Allen is nodding back. He can't believe an investigator would bother coming to a victim's funeral. Why? He's not suspecting him? No way.

The blur which was my funeral is finally over. Mark's been patiently waiting for family and friends to pay their respects to Allen and leave. Allen sees Mark paying respects to me out of corner of his eye, and I can tell it makes him feel uneasy. He's wondering if we knew each other. I hope he doesn't think.

Mark's approaching Allen. *Oh, good. Oh, no.* I should have told him. He's introducing himself as FBI. He's inviting Allen to have coffee. I can tell what Allen is thinking: Holy shit, maybe they do suspect me. But what else is he going to do? He doesn't want to go home. All his family is there helping with Max and cooking and stuff. As much as Allen appreciates their help, he can't handle it all right now. In a strange way, he would rather be interrogated by this stranger than go back to our home. He's daydreaming about how I'd made it such a home. How I'd changed his and Max's lives, too.

As Mark is giving polite condolences, Allen's mind keeps wandering. He's thinking about my parents, how it was probably a good thing they'd gone first. I told him they'd died in a car accident about four years before Allen and I met. He's thinking about Max, and how a parent probably couldn't survive losing a child. He knows he couldn't. Still, he's wishing he had met them. He's wanting to know now, more than ever, where I'd gotten my smile, my green eyes, my crooked toes that I've always hated so much. He would ask them if I'd always been so independent, so stoic, and so strong. Or did something happen to make me such a fighter? He's wondering if they are with me now. This thought consoles him a little.

Back to reality, Sweetie. Mark's got something to tell you.

CHAPTER FOUR

Waffle House, our favorite Sunday morning, throw-on-a-hat, forget-the-makeup breakfast joint. Allen is trying hard to listen as Mark explains, but it's hard. All he can think about is how many fun times we had here. Nothing fancy, just silly laughter and long conversations about art or music or where grits really come from. Had we ever figured that out? Mark's voice brings him out of his daze. "I have some difficult things to tell you, Allen." Allen can feel his heart in his throat. But what could be more difficult than being told your new wife has been shot? He braces himself mentally. "The good news is, we know who did this, and we're hot on his trail."

"The sniper," Allen replies, not believing he is saying it now.

Mark explains, "Our sources have confirmed that it was definitely the work of her ex-husband and..."

"What?" Allen interrupts. "Ex-husband? Sid was married before?"

"Actually, Allen, she was married twice before you met her." Allen can't believe what he's hearing. "The first time she was eighteen years old," Mark continues. "He was a real dirtball. He's the one responsible for her death."

"Not that it matters anymore, but what about the other guy?" Allen asks.

"He died. Apparently, a suicide. It was a fatal shotgun wound to the head."

Allen is stunned. "How could she keep something like that from me? She was married before me? She lied to me? My sweet, new wife? Why? I must admit, I was a bit surprised when I met her that she was a thirty-three year old who hadn't been married or had any children, but she'd moved around so much that...Oh."

Allen is realizing now that there is much more to the story. Although Mark is doing a good job of explaining the facts to Allen, I wish I could be explaining the emotional side of things. My side. Mark is just hitting the basic highlights. Still, Allen is overwhelmed and can't believe what he has just heard. Mark is handing Allen an official-looking business card as they leave the Waffle House, and Allen wonders if he is in some strange dream.

I'm sorry, Sweetie. You should have heard it from me, not some FBI agent. There's so much more to tell you.

"So, what'll it be, Allen?" Allen, still in shock, recognizes the bartender's voice. He can't even bring himself to tell his faithful companion what has happened. After a few, he's not yet drunk. He thinks maybe he'll drink himself to oblivion; maybe he'll stop drinking altogether. I'd wanted him to. Begged him to. He feels sorry. Pictures are flashing through his mind, but he can't grab onto any one of them. He recalls odd things about my actions. How I'd hated crowds, how I would get panicky sometimes, seemingly for no reason at all.

It's called PTSD, sweetheart. Posttraumatic Stress Disorder. Symptoms: insomnia, anxiety, fear, trouble fitting in, nightmares, panic attacks, and so on. It's described as: an unfortunate disturbance of normal psychological processes caused by a horrific event.

He'd thought that my compulsion for changing my hairstyle so often was a little kooky, but maybe it wasn't so kooky after all. A lot of good it did me, though. And the photos...I'd told him that all of my childhood photos had been lost during a move, but had they? He realizes he doesn't recall ever seeing a photo of me from before my life with him and Max. When you add everything up, it makes sense now. He feels sick to his stomach. He's sad and angry. He feels so alone. In a daze, all he wants to do is sleep.

He's home at last. His sisters have been worried, but he just wants to be alone. Heading straight up the stairs, he can't help but think that I'll never again be there to greet him. He wants to scream, "Why, God?" But he's not even ready to go there yet. He'll have a heart-to-heart with God later. Right now, he needs to sleep.

CHAPTER FIVE

Our bedroom. It's usually so warm and cozy, but not today. Or is it tonight, he's wondering. What time is it anyway? When you lose someone you love with all your soul, time just stands still. How do you get past that moment, that very instant when some stranger tells you your new wife has just been killed? Your world stops. At least, that's what Allen had thought. But now his world is morphing into some strange *Twilight Zone* episode featuring snipers and ex-husbands and FBI agents.

Our bedroom. Max had been so eager to help move my things in immediately after our wedding reception. I told him *I* could move in that night, but my *things* could wait a day or two. I've always loved our room. Well, not always. When Allen was still a bachelor, his bedroom décor consisted of a queen-size bed with a king-size headboard and a small TV on an even smaller table. But that was before it became our room. With a woman's touch, it had successfully transformed into a haven. My favorite writing place.

The flowers from my birthday are almost dead. Japanese lilies. My favorite. Allen is thinking about throwing them away. Why do people buy flowers anyway, he's thinking. Maybe he should have bought me flowers more often. Maybe he should have done a lot of things. But how do you know? Looking at our engagement portrait, Allen is filled with the memory of that day. Two artists getting married. How cool is that? Soul mates. He can't believe he didn't really know me. He feels betrayed. Lying on the bed, he realizes it smells like me, and there's no way he'll be able to sleep. With his mind racing, he takes Mark's business card from the nightstand, thumbs it, and stares at the gold FBI seal. He wonders out loud, "Am I asleep?" Maybe this is all a bad dream. Maybe the alarm is about to go off & he'll go to the funeral, where there will be no FBI agents, no secret past, no other husbands. Maybe there was no sniper at all. Maybe he'll wake up & I'll be lying there next to him. Allen loved waking up with me, his favorite time of the day. He's wondering if he ever told me that. Damn.

No, it's real. He's sitting at the desk, realizing it has quite a history. He's realizing I am a part of that history now. Me. History. He feels sick to his stomach again.

The desk belonged to his great-great-grandfather, just after the Civil War. Allen remembers growing up, watching his father spend many hours at that desk, paying bills. He remembers how much pride he felt, seeing me writing at The Desk. He should have told me that. *Should have.* He's thinking, "If I could just relive the last day I saw her sitting here, writing, I would have told her how beautiful she was, flannel pajamas, bunny slippers and all." He always thought of me as so studious and smart. Sometimes he felt like he wasn't good enough for me. He admired me. How I loved to read, write, do crossword and logic puzzles. He never understood how anyone could actually enjoy doing such things, but he admired me just the same.

He's thinking how he knew it was too good to be true. I had seemed so perfect. Perfect for him, anyway. We had not only gotten our degrees from the same university, but went through the same program, under the same instructor. We were both painters. We both loved to cook and travel. We liked the same music and movies. We had everything in common. Or so he'd thought. Maybe it was all a lie, he's thinking.

I wish I could explain. . .

Something in the back of Allen's brain is trying to make its way to the front. He's starting to recall my trouble with school registration, how it took me months and months of paperwork to get enrolled, and it's all starting to make sense now. Maybe I wasn't going through months of filling out paperwork. Maybe I had been afraid to leave a paper trail at all. Somehow, I eventually got in, he realizes. But then I had also dropped out of the education program. "They kept messing up the paperwork," I had told him. He's remembering how upset I was when a fingerprint card was needed, and how funny I acted when he said it was no big deal.

He'd said, "Let's just go do it now," but I came up with some excuse and blew it off. The next thing he knew, I had dropped the program altogether. He now knows why. I was hiding from my past. I had wanted so badly to be a teacher. He thought dropping the program meant I wasn't serious about it, but now he knows that wasn't true. He recalls my way with people, with kids. I was a natural teacher, he's thinking to himself, always sharing and helping others.

He's wondering how much else I gave up. He doesn't even know about the time one of my paintings won a regional contest. First place and best of show out of more than eight hundred entries. Too bad it was a self-portrait. What was I thinking? I hadn't counted on winning; I only entered for the experience. I made it to the national level of the contest, but had to withdraw. The people who made it to the national level were to fly to New Mexico for a press conference and would be featured in a national magazine. Any artist's dream. Why hadn't I painted a landscape like everyone else?

Allen's heart is aching, and he misses me like crazy. We'd lived and worked together, but even when we were apart for one day, we always missed each other. Friends thought we were crazy. They could never have understood what we had. We were best friends. Allen is suddenly feeling unbelievable sadness, realizing he'll miss me forever. How is he going to do this? What if he loses his mind? What about Max?

Too anxious to sleep, he's sitting at The Desk and turning on my computer. Is it wrong to read my stuff now that I'm gone? I had been working on a book. A book. He can't even stand writing a letter, much less a book. He can't believe now that he showed so little interest in my work. Support yes, interest no. He would bring me breakfast in bed and tell me to write. He knew it fed my soul. He loved to see how I glowed when I was creating anything: a painting, a sculpture, a book. He feels so sad now. And guilty. The extent of his interest in my book had been, "Am I in it?" in a joking way. He's thinking to himself, "Everything was a joke to me."

But I like your sense of humor. . .

CHAPTER SIX

He's noticing my journal and feeling an uneasy pang. He's never even dreamed of reading it before. It wasn't so much a privacy thing; he just figured it was girl stuff, like, "I'm having a bad hair day," "I got my period today; what a bummer," etc. It's taking on a whole new meaning now. The journal feels heavy in his hand. Would this hold the truth? This was not just any girl, he's thinking. This was a girl who put a whole group of felons behind bars. Weapons-hoarding, government-hating, white supremacist felons. What do you suppose a girl like that writes in her journal? He's touching the cloth cover, but decides to put it back in it's cubby in the desk.

He's opening a computer file of mine that says simply, "book." He's reading the list of possible titles: *To Hell and Back, Anonymous, Unknown Author,* and finally, *Looking for Snipers.* He almost falls off the chair. If he had achieved any hint of a buzz at the bar, this sobers him right up. It had been right under his nose all the time. He probably would have assumed it was all fiction anyway—I loved my Stephen King novels. He had just bought me one last week, one of the only ones I hadn't read yet, only a couple of bucks at the used book store. But you'd have thought he'd bought me a house. He loved that about me. Simple things. I appreciated the simple things. I guess I know more than most of us how precious life is. If we spend our lives just waiting around for the next big thing to happen, that's how we miss out on all the little things. I was always a fan of the little things. Sometimes, that's all we have.

What had I been through, he's wondering. And all alone, too. Or was I? Were my parents really killed in an accident? Were they murdered as well? Were they still alive, and I just couldn't contact them? And what about that other husband? Was it really a suicide? Maybe they were after Sid, he's thinking. Maybe he came home early and got in the way. Why hadn't I told him? He would have understood, he's assuring himself. He would have kept me safe. Or would he? Maybe he would have weighed the risks and stayed away from me. When do you tell someone something like that? Not on the first date, of course. After you trust them. But by then, you're emotionally involved. The longer you wait, the harder it would be to tell your partner. How do you bring it up? "Oh, honey, by the way, I was a witness for the FBI against my husband when I was eighteen, and now I'm living under an assumed name & hiding to save my life. Would you like some more coffee?"

He's going back to my journal now. It isn't taking long for him to realize it was a resource for my book and was actually written *during* my time on the witness stand. He's not sure if he's ready to comprehend what he's about to read, but he has to know everything. He has to know who his wife really was. He's suddenly realizing the irony of the situation and actually cracking a small smile. I had always encouraged him to read more, said it was good for the mind and the soul. He's finally sitting down with a book, and it's mine. If you could only see me now, he's thinking. He's noticing that the name has been scratched out on the inside cover. This doesn't seem to register. My journal is taking him back in time. "Journal entry..."

CHAPTER SEVEN

Journal entry, 7 November 1990

Well, where do I begin? I have so many terrible memories crowding my mind that I don't always recall them in order. Bringing up one bad memory always reminds me of another. Sometimes I feel like I'm losing my mind. Sometimes I just feel numb. I still can't help blaming myself for the past five years. It was five years ago that I met him. Jack. Just writing his name makes me cringe. Our so-called marriage was legally dissolved three weeks ago today. I'm writing this journal to release some stress, get things straight in my mind, and reassure myself that what I'm doing now is the right thing. God, I hope I'm doing the right thing. Of course, it's the right thing. So much has happened in the past few weeks that I feel like I have to get it down on paper just to keep myself from going crazy.

Allen settles deeper into his chair.

When I try to figure out how I got to this place, I keep going back to my childhood. Sure, my parents worked hard to raise the five of us kids, and even though times were tough, there was always food on the table. They loved us kids more than anything. But there was one big rule: The man of the house is the master. Dad is always right and don't piss him off. I'm not saying it's my father's fault that I'm in this situation now; not at all. But his personality helped form my perception of how men and women react to each other in a marriage, which has became my downfall. After all, when you grow up with a domineering male as a role model, you have no idea that things can be any different. You think it's perfectly acceptable for your husband to treat you like dirt. You think, "This is what being married is like." The woman waits on the man hand and foot, and the man criticizes everything she does. That's normal, right? At first, it was so easy being submissive to Jack. I thought it was what I was supposed to do. I grew up watching my mom do it so well. She is a saint, putting up with my father all these years. I don't blame her one bit; she's just doing what she was raised to do. My parents and their parents before them are from a different generation, when, I guess, women were supposed to be submissive to their husbands. That doesn't mean the women were blind or stupid, not by any means. My mom is one of the smartest ladies I know. She puts up with my dad's antics because she loves him. She may have grown-up without much in the way of material things, but she's amazing. She's strong, intelligent, and beautiful. I got my love of reading from her.

I remember being very sheltered as I was growing up. Even though I was mature for my age, I was kept pretty close to home. I was the youngest of the five children, so maybe it was hard for my parents to change with the times and let their baby girl go out of their sight. Maybe the times have changed so much that there was a lot more to worry about with me. When I was a little girl, I was very close to my father, handing him tools and working on projects with him. I loved working in his workshop or going to his job site. It sounds funny, but I loved the smells. Wood, metal, oil. They all mingled to create one distinct aroma that meant one thing: time with dad. I was daddy's little girl. But as I got older and started to have opinions and ideas of my own, that's when we started to grow apart. Dad's way was the only way. The older I got, the more I saw him for what he was, a closed-minded, controlling, bitter person. As I watched him through fresh eyes, I grew to hate the way he was and especially, the way he treated my mom.

I was a good kid and never got into drinking or drugs or any other kind of trouble that teenagers get into. I loved school, I loved to draw, and I loved playing my violin. But things began to change. I got to the point where I hated going home. My dad was so negative that I just couldn't stand to be around him. I mostly hated the way he treated my mom. I started to go on dates with boys just to get out of the house. Boys who were trying to become men would pressure me to have sex with them. I wasn't planning on having sex before marriage, so I wouldn't go out with the same boy too many times. The more dates you went on with a boy, the more they expected from you. It didn't take long to figure that one out. I did fall into what I thought was love and found myself with a steady boyfriend.

Charlie. The inevitable happened and Charlie dumped me for refusing to "put out." I thought my life was over. Stupid little girl. I became depressed and angry, and my grades began to fall. Charlie lived on our street, and I watched him arm in arm with his new girlfriend. I watched as my father criticized my mother, and soon his criticism spilled over onto me. I just wanted his approval and love. I know he loved me, but I just couldn't see it at the time. It was a crucial time in my teenage life when I was forming my own perspective on life, relationships, sex, and love.

I was sixteen when I left home.

I went to live with distant family, which seemed like a good idea at the time. I did well in school, but I was ready to be done with it. My new school was just beginning to teach subjects that my old school had covered two years earlier. My senior year was like doing time. I was ready to get on with my life, ready to be all grown-up. Then it happened. Being raped by a family member has a way of making you grow up fast.

Once again, I found myself needing to run away.

Allen is remembering I'd always had some excuse not to visit my family...

UNKNOWN AUTHOR

CHAPTER EIGHT

Journal entry, 14 November 1990

Then there was Jack. I had met him while visiting my sister who was stationed at Ft. Jackson in South Carolina. My young heart thought it was in love. Again. Stupid, stupid little girl. Now I realize I was just suffering from low self-esteem and would have welcomed any attention. Jack was a Green Beret, and to a sheltered teenager, that made him my knight in shining armor. Between the criticism of my father and the rape of another man, I felt like damaged goods. Even though Jack treated me with no respect whatsoever, I thought I was lucky to have him. I did whatever he wanted; I changed the way I walked, talked, ate, and acted. I became his property. Although I see clearly now that how he'd treated me was wrong, I was completely blind at the time. That's why when he said he loved me and asked me to marry him; I was thrilled.

It was miserable from day one. I spent our wedding night crying on the bathroom floor. Maybe I thought I deserved to be treated badly. I'd never really thought about it that way until just now, but maybe I did. He criticized everything about me, and I believed him. A friend once told me the bad stuff is so much easier to believe than the good stuff. How true. One day he would tell me I didn't wear enough makeup, and the next day he would tell me I was wearing too much. He would criticize things I couldn't change, like the size of my feet or the color of my eyes. He constantly told me I was a fat cow, and even made me prepare meals for him and then watch him eat while I starved. He controlled every single move I made. I became anorexic and had no idea until years later when other people told me. I should have known when I had to special-order size zero jeans from Sears that something wasn't normal. Amazingly, I still saw myself as fat. I would come home in my size zero jeans, and Jack would say, "Keep at it and maybe someday you'll lose all that baby fat of yours."

Allen is remembering how touchy Sid had been about her weight.

I started to see myself through his eyes and started hating everything I saw. He convinced me I was disgusting and pathetic, and no one would ever love me. I should have asked myself, if I was so disgusting, what did he want with me? But I was well beyond logical thought by then. It's funny how quickly brainwashing can take effect. He showed me how he expected the bed to be made with perfect military corners, and if I didn't do it up to his standards, he would drag me by the arm into the bedroom, tear the bed apart, and make me do it over. He had complete power over me.

The more he criticized, the worse my self-esteem became. The worse I felt about myself, the more I thought I needed him. Sick, huh? I became so devoted to him that no matter what he demanded, I eagerly jumped. I now know what the word submissive really means. I've also come to realize that I never really loved him; I was just in love with the idea of being married—of having someone. I thought being alone would mean something was wrong with me. I showed him kindness and respect, and he treated me like dirt.

He knew all the tricks, though. Whenever I would start to question any-thing, he would tell me, "You're just a stupid kid; you don't know anything." He was eleven years older than me. His favorite word became "immature." He would proposition other women right in front of me, and if I said anything, he would say I was simply being immature. He said I would grow out of it. He led me to believe that if I was a "real" woman, it wouldn't bother me. Of course I wanted to be a real woman, so I would hold my hurt feelings inside. I began to learn how to keep my mouth shut. . .and my eyes. One time we were in the mall, and I saw him flirting with another woman. When I approached them and said it was time to go, he rolled his eyes and said, "little sisters." I figured if I had been prettier or thinner, that maybe he wouldn't flirt with other women. Once he told me that he'd just slept with his ex-girlfriend before coming home to me. I was devastated. When I asked him why, he smugly said, "Because she was there." I knew by then that I didn't love him, but I didn't know what to do. I felt numb. I felt lost. I felt so alone. I couldn't go back home. I was too ashamed to tell anyone what was going on. After all, I'd gotten myself into it.

CHAPTER NINE

Journal entry, 21 November 1990

Jack was totally obsessed with weapons. Every spare minute he had, he spent shooting. Every penny we earned, he spent on guns and ammunition. He even did his own bullet reloading so he could control, to the grain, how much gunpowder was in each bullet. Sometimes he made me do his reloading if he had errands to run. Of course, he warned me that they had to be done perfectly. If a bullet didn't seem to pack the punch that he expected at the shooting range, of course it was my fault. I still have a scar on my thumb where I accidentally got it caught in one of the reloading presses.

Allen had been meaning to ask Sid about that scar (and all the others).

He competed in matches where everyone shot at silhouette targets of scaled-down animals. At first I thought it was for fun, but he took it way too seriously. He made me spot for him, and if I said he'd missed high, he would say, "That's impossible because I was aiming low."

After a few times, I would say, "Fine, I won't spot for you then." This made him furious, and he would yell at me in front of everyone. The men thought it was good that he was keeping me in line, and most of their wives were too afraid to say anything. This gave them all a good laugh.

I gradually made friends with one of the wives, Carrie, who changed my life without even knowing it. Jack usually kept me away from other people (the better to control you, my dear), but while he was competing, Carrie would talk to me. She was about ten years older than I was, and she had a world of experiences compared to me. I may have been stuck in a horrible marriage with no happiness in sight, but she said something I will never forget. I don't even think it completely registered until much later, but it did. Out of the blue one day, she said, "You know, you don't have to be treated like that. It's not normal the way he treats you." At first, I was dumbfounded. I remember thinking, how does she know how he treats me? He was tame in public compared to what went on behind closed doors. But then she probably knew that as well. I may not have thanked her at that moment, but her words came back to me later and gave me the strength that I needed.

It wasn't long before the abuse got more and more physical. He started doing scary things, weird things. Between his innate cruelty and his Special Forces training, this made him very dangerous. At first, I didn't know just how dangerous. I thought he was just being macho, showing off. He would do things like put his thumb and index finger on my neck and say, "You know, I could kill you before you could make a sound." He constantly boasted about his ability to make people disappear without anyone knowing he was involved and to make "accidents" happen when he wasn't even in the same country. At that time, I thought he was watching too many Chuck Norris movies. I thought it was all talk. Now I know better.

Once I took a second too long to get him a beer. He must have thrown the bottle pretty hard because it felt like a sledge hammer in the middle of my back. The impact caused me to hit the floor and the beer to go all over the kitchen. He ordered me to get down on my hands and knees and he held me by the neck while I cleaned it up. He called me a bitch. He did all of this in front of another Green Beret, who just laughed. To this day, I still hate the smell of beer.

Journal entry, 6 December 1990

One of my vivid memories started out as an act of seduction. Jack became amorous, kissing my neck and touching me and slowly removed my clothes. He had me lay back on the bed, nude and waiting. His next move seemed to come from nowhere. He opened the drawer of the nightstand and removed a combat knife. I started to sit up, but before I knew it, he was on top of me. Somehow, with one hand, he grabbed both of my wrists and slammed them above my head. He put his face about an inch from mine and stared into my eyes with a coldness I'll never forget. If he was playing a game, I didn't want to piss him off and turn it into something serious. If this wasn't a game, I knew I didn't have a prayer *of getting away. Still holding my hands above my head, he sat up on top of me and started following the contours of my body with the knife. He started at my neck, working his way down. He circled the knife blade around my breasts as if he were contemplating the best way in which to carve them. He took the tip of the blade and pushed down on my nipples. Tears started to stream down the sides of my face. Knowing how much he hated the sight of weakness, I tried to laugh it off. He wasn't laughing. Suddenly, he held the blade across my neck and looked into my eyes like he was waiting to see what they would do as he slit my throat. Then he simply stood up, put the knife back into the drawer, and walked away. We never spoke of it.*

Allen realizes his hands are shaking. He's shamefully remembering the time when I had a panic attack because he tried putting my arms over my head.

He would do things like twist my arm until just before the point of breaking it, and when I would cry, he would say, "See, you're such a wimp. You'll never amount to anything." He made me take apart weapons and put them back together while he timed me. Of course, I was never fast enough for his standards. He taught me what Russian roulette was, the hard way.

Amazingly, he allowed me to join the Army Reserves. I wanted to join the Regular Army, but he said no way. He didn't want me becoming too independent. I guess he figured in the reserves I would still be at home, under his control. I later found out the only reason he let me join is because he honestly thought I wouldn't even make it through basic training. The day I left for basic, he said, "You'll never make it. You'll come home crying to me."

I hated him.

CHAPTER TEN

Journal entry, 10 December 1990

I was one of those few people who actually enjoyed basic training. Heck, it was nothing compared to living with Jack. I already knew how to wear a uniform, what the ranks were, how to polish boots. I was very familiar with making beds the military way, going without food, and, of course, weapons.

There we were, the first week of basic, sitting along a curb. Our orders: take your M-16 apart and raise your hand. Once the drill sergeant says , "Go, put it back together and raise your hand again," I simply did what I was told, and when my M-16 was back together, the drill sergeant approached me. As I looked around, I saw that all the other soldiers were still struggling to take their weapons apart. He suspiciously said, "Private, have you ever handled an M-16 before?"

"No, Drill Sergeant," I lied.

On another occasion, we were at the firing range, shooting at paper targets. We were paired-up with our bunk buddies, and we were to take turns shooting and spotting for each other. My bunk buddy had sprained her ankle, so our company commander said he would spot for me. I was so nervous. He never even came near us, much less spotted for us at the firing range. The drill was, fire five rounds, have your spotter go downrange and check your target, then fire five more at a time. After I fired my first five rounds, my company commander went downrange. After meticulously studying my target, he walked back toward me, shaking his head the whole way. I was so embarrassed. I knew I was nervous, but had I missed the target altogether? He said, "Private, where did you learn to shoot?" I was too afraid to answer. He laughed and said, "I could cover all five of your shots with a dime!" Still, I didn't tell him where or how I'd learned to shoot. I left it at, "Thank you, Sir."

Journal entry, 13 December 1990

While I was about to graduate from basic training at Ft. McClellan,

Alabama, Jack was finishing Warrant Officer Training at Ft. Rucker, Alabama. Not far away. He was supposed to come pick me up and drive me to airborne school. Just before graduating from basic, I had a small accident.

There was this part of the obstacle course that resembled the monkey bars you see in a playground. Only these monkey bars were made of logs and stood twenty-five feet above the ground. And instead of crossing underneath them, hand-over-hand, we had to run on top of them. I can still picture it, running across those logs, not a care in the world, when my foot slipped. I fell, straddling a log, and suffered a stress-fracture in my lower pelvis. The alternative was to tumble over the side, falling twenty-five feet to the ground, so I considered myself lucky at the time. I reluctantly called Jack to tell him I probably wouldn't graduate on time, figuring he would have a good laugh. He was furious. He said, "Do you know how embarrassing it's going to be telling my buddies that my wife couldn't even make it through basic training?"

So I made it.

During this same phone call, he informed me that he wouldn't be driving me to airborne school, anyway. He said there wasn't time. He was only forty minutes away from me, and I knew he had ten days of leave. Then he said he just wanted to get back to Ft. Jackson. We hadn't seen each other in over two months. That stupid little girl in me felt hurt for a moment, but then my hurt turned to anger. I used my anger to help me grow.

One of my drill sergeants found out I wouldn't have a ride to airborne school and asked me why. I explained, embarrassed, and I never dreamed he would do anything about it. Somehow, he got a hold of Jack, and somehow, he convinced him to come get me. I was afraid Jack would be mad.

When Jack picked me up, he said, "I saw a girl coming around the corner on crutches, and I was relieved to see that it wasn't you." Just when I was about to say, "How sweet," he continued. . ."I would have turned right around and left you here. I'd be embarrassed to be seen with you on crutches." He was so obsessed with appearances that he used to say, "When you get pregnant, I'm sending you to live with my mother; I don't want to have to look at you when you get that fat." He would say, "You're the one who wants a kid, so you can deal with it." Little did he know, I had already decided I would never have a child with him. I hated him. But I was scared. I had nowhere to go.

By the time he dropped me off at Ft. Benning for airborne school, I knew I was a different person and needed to start thinking about my own survival. I became tough. Not only physically, but mentally. I still can't explain how I made it through basic training with a stress-fractured pelvis, but my newfound tough-ness wasn't enough to get me through airborne school. When the airborne instruc-tors say, "feet and knees together," they really mean it. That's what I failed to do during a particularly hard landing, sporting more than half my weight in equipment as I jumped. I knew instantly that I was in trouble. I don't remember feeling pain right away, just anger. I was seriously pissed-off. I knew I wasn't going to earn my wings anytime soon. I remember thinking to myself that I had done some major damage to my bottom-half. I just didn't know how much dam-age. I started to stand up, and then I knew. I remember my mind speeding up. I remember feeling confused. The sky and trees were moving, but they weren't spinning like you'd expect them to be just before you pass out. They seemed to be closing in on me. Then everything went black. The next thing I remember is waking up in an Army hospital, being criticized by a warrant officer/doctor guy. He was telling me (in a less-than-friendly tone of voice) that I had screwed up my entire life. He said I would be put out of the Army on a medical discharge, I would probably never have children, and I would be in a wheelchair for the rest of my life. I didn't say a word to him, but in my mind, I said, like hell.

It was dark and depressing in there. I don't even remember what all was done to me; it's like a big ugly blur. They eventually sent me back to Ft. Jackson to continue healing. I became a regular at Patterson Army Hospital and grew to hate that place. No one was ever happy to be there, not the patients or the staff.

Jack reveled in the realization that he could say, "I told you so." He didn't even acknowledge that I had made it through basic training with a stress-fractured pelvis. When friends would ask how my training went, he would tell them I washed out. Being a "wash out" in the military means you're a failure, *you couldn't cut it, you're weak. Although I was miserable at the thought of not earning my wings, and by earning my wings, I mean more than the metal things they pin on your chest upon completion of airborne school, I didn't care what he and his friends thought, anymore. I was changing inside. I was better than any of them. I just had to convince myself to believe it.*

Allen is shaking his head, starting to see how I'd gotten to be so tough.

CHAPTER ELEVEN

Journal entry, 20 December 1990

Still, I tried everything to make it work. The problem was, Jack saw no problem. The more I tried to be open and grow, the more he oppressed me. Whenever I did something good, he told me all the bad things about me and dragged me down. I completed almost two years of college. I was working full-time and paying my own way. He made it so hard for me to study. I think he felt threatened. I think he didn't want me to gain my independence. He was like a child. Every five minutes, he would make me go get him a drink, or make him a sandwich, or go to the store. When I would finally get on a roll with my studying, he would turn the TV up as loud as it would go, then just give me a look that said, "Go ahead and say something; I dare you." I did the best I could for as long as I could, but then I just gave up. It became too much to fight. I made a promise to myself I would get my degree someday. No matter what.

He tried the same stunt at DLI as well. The Defense Language Institute. The 5th Special Forces Group was moving to Ft. Campbell, Kentucky, and Jack didn't want to go. He was able to switch to the 7th Group, but had to go to DLI at The Presidio of Monterey, in California, to learn Spanish. One of the soldiers didn't show up, so there was an empty slot for the class. It is tradition at DLI to offer empty slots to students' spouses, figuring they can practice together, which, in turn, can make the student do even better. So they let me take the course. Even though it wasn't necessary for my military job, my Commander at Ft. Jackson thought it would be a productive way to spend my time while continuing to heal from my accident. I was of no use to my Unit until I could jump again.

For the first time, Jack and I were in the same situation. Of course, he boasted about how much better he was going to do in the class—until the work actually began. I saw the Mighty Jack in a whole new light. He wasn't so strong after all. It was an intensive, six-month course, and he failed out within the first month. I almost felt sorry for him. Almost. We tried at first to do our homework together, but he would argue with every single answer I came up with. He would yell at me and call me stupid, while writing his own answers. I would say, "Okay, but I'm not changing mine." He said he couldn't wait to prove me wrong. He failed every quiz and the first big test before they dropped him from the class.

Feeling threatened again, he tried everything to make me quit. But I was a different girl this time. I started doing what was best for me. We had picked up our lives and driven all the way across the country, and I wasn't about to leave empty-handed. Despite his attempts to make me quit, I graduated cum laude. I was considered fluent in Spanish by the U.S. Military, and I felt good about myself for the first time.

Allen is realizing he didn't really know me at all. He's thinking to himself, "Sid spoke Spanish? Who knew?"

Having no reason to study, Jack spent his whole time in Monterey shooting his weapons. DLI was very stressful, not to mention dealing with Jack, so I spent every evening sitting on the rocks, watching the sun set over the ocean. I loved to listen to the sea lions and otters and breathe the salty air. In retrospect, I'm surprised he allowed me to do this, but I'm sure it kept me out of his way while he did whatever he wanted. It may sound cliché, but those nights I spent in Monterey changed my life. Spending time with yourself is a good way to learn who you really are. It was the beginning of me becoming me.

Journal entry, 27 December 1990

On our way back from Monterey, Jack learned he had received a phone call from Washington. He had a choice. He could leave right away for Panama without me (these were dangerous times), or he could go in two years and take me with him. He left right away. No discussion. That's the way life was with Jack. Sometimes I would find out about major decisions he'd made, ones that affected us both, by overhearing him tell a buddy of his. My opinion wasn't important to him. He certainly didn't see me as his equal.

Things just got worse between us. Right up until he boarded the plane, he *was a total jerk. The day he left, he spent our last two hours together sitting on a bar stool in the airport, talking weapons with some guy who was going with him. He was going to be gone for a year. I was his wife. He acted as if I didn't even exist. Then he left. I had mixed feelings. I was relieved that he wouldn't be there to abuse me, but I was still afraid to be alone. It turns out I wouldn't be.*

Jack didn't want to be paying rent at Ft. Jackson while he was in Panama (even though the military gave him money for both since he was married), so he arranged for me to stay with a shooting buddy's wife. Turns out, it was Carrie. Jack assured me that staying with Carrie would allow us to save money to buy a house when he returned. I knew better, but I had no choice in the matter. I now know he spent all of our military housing allowance on weapons. Big surprise.

Carrie and I became eternal friends. She was so strong. She was the kind of woman who made her own mayonnaise and hand-stitched quilts, but she had also been a soldier. We laughed and cried and talked about anything and everything. Her strength continued to feed my desire for strength. Without knowing it, she became my mentor. To this day, I thank God for her. Her husband had been sent to Korea, so she and their kids and I became like family. We helped each other cope. I studied her. She was the kind of person I wanted to be.

CHAPTER TWELVE

Journal entry, 3 January 1991

As time went on, Jack told me how badly he was suffering in Panama. He said he was in the middle of nowhere, and it was barely civilized. I actually felt bad for him. I did odd jobs around town and saved money for months. He said that he missed me like crazy, and I thought maybe he was changing. I thought maybe he'd realized what a marriage was supposed to be like. I thought maybe the distance made him realize that he appreciated me. I bought a plane ticket with the money I'd saved and flew to Panama for eight days. He said he couldn't wait to see me, and that he wouldn't be able to keep his hands off of me.

But then I arrived. He didn't hug me. He didn't kiss me. He didn't even carry my suitcase. He acted as if I were some guy he was hired to pick up from the airport. Since my flight arrived late that evening, we were staying in a hotel in Panama City instead of going all the way to the house where he was staying. Despite the lack of clear, hot water and the occasional loss of electricity, the hotel was pretty fancy. It was the Panama City Hilton and was as nice as any hotel I'd ever stayed in. It was grand and beautiful. The courtyard was filled with tropical plants and hand-painted tiles. The employees wore perfectly pressed suits and actually walked around with white towels over one arm, like in the movies. I thought about Jack's claim of being stuck in the middle of nowhere—hardly civilized—he had said. But I quickly dismissed the thought, figuring the next day, I would see where he was having to live, which could be light years away from where we stayed that night.

I reluctantly took a cold shower and slipped into a silk nightgown, which just happened to be Jack's favorite color. Maybe this would be our new begin-ning. Stupid little girl. He was watching TV and wouldn't even look at me. The power went off. I thought, what great timing; how romantic! He just sat there. Not a word. Not a movement. He wouldn't even answer me when I asked him what was wrong. The power came back on, including the TV. What was going on? What was all that talk about missing me and not being able to take his hands off of me? Why had he begged me to come there?

SIDNEY

The next day, I saw how he was "suffering." He was living in a gorgeous house with a tropical garden. And hardly civilized? There were cafes, grocery stores, and a movie theatre. It was a nice town. He started showing me all the new stuff he had bought. Another video camera, a third VCR, another TV, another CD player. (What happened to buying a house?) As if he'd read my mind, he announced that he'd decided we wouldn't be buying a house. He said an apartment would be cheaper, and that way, he could buy more weapons. Was he trying to get me to leave him? Of course not. I forgot, that wasn't an option with Jack.

I was so sick of his obsession. We always went shooting on our anniversary, my birthday, Thanksgiving, even Christmas Day. He couldn't take seven days of leave for a honeymoon, but he sure didn't hesitate to take seven days off to go to a state shooting match. He spent all kinds of time and money on the match, buying just the right gun and measuring every grain of gunpowder so he could be a serious contender. It turns out, he was way out of his league. It wasn't enough to make him quit, though. I thought Panama would be the one place where I wouldn't see an NRA shooting match. I was wrong. Guess where he took me the second day of my visit?

On the third day, we went snorkeling from one island to another. We were truly in the middle of nowhere. We had rented a Jeep, driven through the jungle, and paid a man with no legs to give us a boat ride to the first island. I couldn't help but notice that even though he had to walk with his hands, dragging his torso along the beach, he was happy. With his thatch hut and giggling little kids hovering around him, he was a happy man. I could see it in his eyes. I wanted to be happy someday.

I wondered how he would know when to pick us up, but I figured he did this all the time. It could have been wonderful. I was scared to death of open waters, but I believe the best way to overcome a fear is to face it head on. I was glad we were doing something adventurous together, something different. I was in awe of the crystal clear water and the coral and exotic fish. I saw parrot fish, angel fish, and huge sting rays, as big as I was. I have to admit, those did make me a little nervous, but they were amazing just the same.

We were halfway between the two islands, in extremely deep water, and my mask filled up with water. I stopped and started to clear my mask. I wanted to do it quickly and move on because I couldn't tread water for long. Jack was SCUBA qualified through the military, so I felt safe enough. But then he started yelling stuff at me, as if I were drowning and needed help. At first it startled me, but then I was just confused. I was fine; I was ready to move on. But he just kept yelling at me, like some kind of lunatic. I realized I was getting tired of treading water, but when I tried to move, he pushed me down. I instinctively grabbed for him, but he kept pushing my hands away. Now I was scared. Was this just one of his mind games, so he could prove I was weaker than he was? Was it some sick test? Was this just fodder so he could tell his buddies what a wimp I was? Whatever his motives, I was terrified. The more I tried to calm down and gain control, the more he yelled and pushed me away. Why was he doing this to me? It seemed to last forever, and I don't even remember how we got back to the first island.

I had had it. The rest of my visit was spent in the house where he and his roommate lived. He expected me to cook, clean, and wait on him and his roommate. I went along with the game. I was just biding my time. One night as I was handing him his dinner, I started to tell him how things were going back home. He said, "Shut up; I can't hear the TV." He was watching a rerun of Miami Vice that I had seen him watch at least twice before. That was it. It was over. I realized that things would never get better. I went upstairs. After his show was over, he came upstairs and asked, "When did you leave?"

I said, "I want a divorce." He simply laughed at me. I kept telling him I wanted a divorce, and he kept telling me he wouldn't give me one.

I returned to the States.

CHAPTER THIRTEEN

Journal entry, 10 January 1991

I would call Jack in an attempt to handle the situation as adults. I actually had a general power of attorney I used for taking care of his bills and stuff while he was gone. I had his truck, his checking account number, and the keys to his storage locker. I could have done whatever I wanted with his stuff, legally. I could have really screwed him over, but I didn't. That wasn't my style. Besides, I didn't want anything from him. I just wanted out. He would call me and beg for three or four hours to give him another chance. He would accuse me of seeing someone else and would demand to know who it was. Surely I couldn't be divorcing him because of any shortcoming of his. He thought he was perfect. He would cry and say that he couldn't live without me. What a joke. Deep down, I think he knew he would never find another woman who would love him. But that wouldn't be enough to make a man like Jack beg. There was another reason he wouldn't let me go. A much bigger reason.

Allen, trying to absorb it all, is rubbing his eyes. His eyes are tired and red, and he's starting to distrust the things they're telling him. He takes a short break, but is compelled to keep reading my journal.

UNKNOWN AUTHOR

CHAPTER FOURTEEN

Journal entry, 17 January 1991

The year we were married, Jack and his best buddy Dale committed a felony. I witnessed the before, I witnessed the after, and to my horror, Jack filled me in on every detail. He and Dale had discussed it a few days before. I was there for the whole conversation. I, of course, assumed that they were just joking, but there was something about Dale's demeanor that worried me. He was nervous. I thought maybe Jack was just testing Dale, wanting to see how far he could make him go. Dale kept saying, "I've got a wife and kids to worry about, man. I can't do anything to screw that up. I don't want to go to jail." Jack seemed to be enjoying his position as the leader, the brave one. He laughed at Dale and assured him that nothing would go wrong. They were both obsessed with weapons, especially military weapons, and they always wanted more. They both wanted to be able to "survive and defend themselves if we were ever invaded." They plotted to take over the government "if the shit ever hit the fan." They were always saying things like, "If I could only get my hands on an M-60..." or "I would sure like to have a grenade launcher." I'd always assumed it was just macho talk—until that night.

About eight p.m., Jack put on his camouflage uniform and started to pack a bag. He put in a black ski mask, a pair of black gloves, some duct tape, and an UZI or a MAC-10, I'm not sure which one it was. I do know he owned both, and this one had a silencer on it. I begged him not to go. I figured he was just going to drive around Ft. Jackson, spying on soldiers in the field. He and Dale did that sometimes. I thought it was weird, but I figured it was just some guy thing to make them feel tough. But this time, he was taking an automatic weapon with a silencer and a ski mask. Even if they were just playing a game, they could get into serious trouble if caught with gear like that. But something in my gut told me this was no longer a game. I remembered how nervous Dale had been a few nights before when they were talking about their plan. Again, I begged Jack not to go. I reminded him that Dale didn't even want to go, and he shouldn't go involving him in something that might get him into trouble. I said that even if our marriage meant nothing to him, he had his career to think about. I thought for sure that would make him think twice. He'd been in the Army for thirteen years, and he'd won all kinds of awards. The Army saw him as a good soldier. So far. He assured me that they wouldn't be seen, and that they were just going to "check things out." Dale showed up at our apartment, acting nervous and avoiding eye contact with me. I tried to get him to change Jack's mind, but he wouldn't even talk to me, and Jack told me to stay out of it. He and Dale left around ten p.m. Finally, I went to bed.

Around two in the morning, I heard Jack come into the bedroom. I pretended to be asleep; I was still mad at him for going. I got up when I heard him in the bathroom, vomiting and crying. I was scared. I asked if there was anything I could do, but he just told me to leave him alone. A little while later, he sat on the side of the bed and told me every detail.

He told me that he and Dale sat in the woods, watching a unit of soldiers who were on a field exercise. They saw an anti-tank weapon that they really wanted, but it was well guarded. While they were sitting there, two soldiers carrying water cans started to walk right by them. This wasn't part of the plan, but they improvised. Jack and Dale stepped out in front of them and told them to drop the water cans. The soldiers thought it was just a game, part of the field exercise. Jack fired two or three rounds into one of the water cans and said, "That's just to let you know the bullets are real. . .and silenced." They dropped the water cans. Jack and Dale tied the guys back to back and put tape on their mouths, all the way around their heads. They seized the soldiers' M-16s. Jack went on to tell me that while he was taping one soldier's hands behind his back, he pushed the barrel of his weapon into the guy's back, and the guy said, "Please don't kill me. I have kids." I felt like vomiting. He said Dale made some comment to the soldiers about this being the work of a white supremacy group, and they left. I thought it was a strange comment to make, but I figured Dale was just trying to throw them off their trail. Blame it on a white supremacy group so they'll never suspect it was the work of their own fellow soldiers.

Jack sat on the side of the bed crying and shaking and saying, "I can't believe what I've done." I was really scared. I had never seen him like this. But the next morning was a completely different story. He sat on the couch, admiring his newly acquired toy. When the story was aired on the news, he took pride in correcting anything they said wrong about the incident. He made me hold "his" M-16 while he ground off the serial number and the U.S. govt. engraving. My hands felt so dirty. Then he painted over the ground area to match the rest of the weapon. I hated that he did it, but I couldn't change it.

Allen is stunned. He's never even held a gun, much less a stolen, military, automatic rifle.

It was that day that Jack first threatened my life specifically. He said that if I ever told anyone, or if I ever tried to leave him, that he would kill me or have a buddy kill me. He said that he and Dale had made an agreement: if Dale's wife or I ever turned them in, they would get revenge for each other. Jack would kill Dale's wife, and Dale would kill me. He said he had plenty of friends who would cover for him and Dale if they had to. People owed him favors. They both agreed they would even kill a cop before going to jail. He said if they ever did go to jail, that they would do everything it took to escape. Jack said he would spend every minute planning his escape and his revenge. Since Dale and Jack were both Green Berets, with extensive training in survival, escape, and evasion, I believed him.

Allen's mind is being flooded with memories now; things are really starting to make sense. He had thought I was a little quirky in my actions and reactions to things. Now he's beginning to understand why.

CHAPTER FIFTEEN

Journal entry, 24 January 1991

I was terrified of my husband. Plain and simple. I had believed for a long time that leaving was not an option, so I tried my best to keep the peace. But I matured and realized that leaving might mean death, but staying would be worse than death. What kind of life was this? Not the kind of life I wanted. So after my visit to Panama, I knew I had to stay strong. I would use the distance to my advantage. I was afraid of him, but at least I wouldn't have to face him. I filed for divorce. When Jack got the papers, he did something unexpected. He became very friendly. He said he would sign the papers without a fight and, hopefully, that would prove to me that he could be a good man. I don't think he knew what a good man was. He helped arrange a quick divorce in his home state of Florida, but said we would both have to appear on the court date. I wasn't quite sure if I believed him, but I didn't know what else to do. He said he would do anything to prove that he could change. He said he hoped to rebuild our relationship from scratch. His words made me sick. But I went along with it, pretending to be gullible, all the while knowing I never wanted to see him again.

Surprisingly, he came home on leave to talk about the divorce. He was so nice. Too nice. He said he would support me until I came back to him. He said he would buy me a car. I had been driving his truck while he was in Panama because my car was totaled when a drunk driver ran me off the road a few months before. It was a hit and run. We actually went car shopping together, found a reasonably priced used car, and Jack got a loan from the bank. Under different circumstances, I might have felt guilty, except for the fact that he'd spent the insurance money from my accident on weapons.

Jack spent the whole week being nice to me, taking me to the movies, and out to dinner. He was like a different person. The old me would have fallen for his act, but I didn't trust him for one second. What I didn't know was, the whole time he was pretending to be there for me, he was setting me up behind my back. His last night there, he came to Carrie's house, where I was still staying. He informed me that he had changed the lock on the storage locker, had cancelled the loan, cancelled the car, and drawn all the money out of our joint checking account. He then informed me that he was going to take his truck to his parents' house in Florida and fly back to Panama from there. That was the real reason he flew home. He had loose ends to tie up. Carrie was out of town visiting her husband in Korea. One last time, Jack threatened me not to leave him. He left me there with no money and no transportation. But before he left, he went through what little stuff I owned, "to try to find evidence against me." After finding nothing, he left.

I called my only other local friend, Liz, and asked her to give me a ride to a pawnshop. It felt good handing them my wedding ring, even though I knew I was getting next to nothing for it. It was symbolic for me, especially since it was Jack's favorite pawnshop for buying weapons. They recognized me, but asked no questions.

When Carrie returned from Korea, she decided she didn't want me staying in their house anymore. She was angry that Jack had invaded their house, which I could understand, and she was afraid that he might return. I didn't blame her one bit, but what was I going to do? Here I was, an officer's wife, with no money, no transportation, and no place to live. And Jack was getting extra money from the Army for being married to me. Liz said I could stay with her. Her husband was in Saudi Arabia, so she let me use his truck as well. But she said I could only stay for two weeks. She was due to have her second child, and her mother was coming to stay. Besides, she was afraid of Jack, just like everyone else. She had even talked me into writing a letter before he came home on leave. She knew that Jack had threatened me about what I knew, and she knew it was something illegal, but she didn't know what it was. But we both expected him to be violent about the divorce, and she wanted me to make it known that if anything happened to me, it was his fault. I wrote a letter explaining that I was afraid for my life, and why Jack had threatened me. I wrote every detail about the crime. I addressed it to CID, the Criminal Investigation Division of the Army. Although nothing violent happened during Jack's visit, the letter would prove to come in handy later. Liz is another friend whose guidance has helped me survive.

CHAPTER SIXTEEN

Journal entry, 1 February 1991

After my two weeks were up at Liz's house, I was planning to move to California to be with one of my sisters. She was going to college there while her husband was stationed in Germany. I was to stay with my friend for two weeks, and the divorce hearing was in Florida in three weeks. I had enough money for a hotel at Ft. Jackson, but by the time I paid for that, plus airfare and a rental car for the trip to Florida for the divorce, I was going to be pushing it to make it all the way to California on what I had left.

I found out that I could work full-time at the Army Reserve Center, where I was stationed for up to two weeks for some extra pay. I was eager to work and keep my mind off of things, but I must have looked like a real wreck. A friend of mine at the Reserve Center asked me what was wrong. I told her that I had filed for a divorce, and that Jack had left me with nothing. I told her that I would be just fine, and that I was just stressed out. She told our commander. I couldn't believe it. I was so ashamed. The commander called me into her office and shut the door. I thought she was going to lecture me about bringing my personal problems to work. She was angry all right, but not with me. She said that Jack had no right to be withholding money from me, and as a soldier, he could be punished for doing so. I told her I didn't want him punished, that I just wanted to get away from him. She took charge and called Jack's commanding officer in Panama. She put him on speakerphone so I could be in on the whole conversation. She informed his commander that Jack was collecting extra money for being married to me, but was leaving me stranded back here in the States. I'll never forget his words. He said, "There's no way I'm going to let some little gold-digging bitch mess with one of my top soldiers." I was stunned. I sat there, silenced. My commander assured Jack's commander that she would be pursuing further action, and they both hung up. Compassionately, she started telling me something, I don't even know what, and then something inside of me snapped. I told her everything. The abuse, the ski mask, the stolen weapons, the threats.

Before I even realized it, she had made a call and two CID agents were knocking on her office door. I began telling them the whole story when they stopped me. They decided to take me to the FBI station. That's when the whirlwind began, and my life was about to change forever.

Jack always said he would kill me if I turned him in or left him; well, now I was doing both. And I was scared. There was no doubt in my mind that he would kill me.

For the next week, I spent almost every day at the CID and FBI offices, answering questions and making statements. They searched Jack's storage locker and found all kinds of illegal stuff, but no M-16s. At first, I was worried they wouldn't find enough evidence to arrest him, but it turns out I knew details about the night of the crime that had not been released to the public. They knew I was telling the truth, but they still hadn't found the weapons that would link him to that particular crime. Moving the M-16s from the storage locker must have been one of the loose ends he had to tie up when he was home on leave.

CHAPTER SEVENTEEN

Journal entry, 15 February 1991

Nothing can quite prepare you for becoming a Federal informant against your husband. I expected the obvious questions concerning Jack's weapons and that night he and Dale stole the M-16s, but the questions just kept coming. The agents were desperate to find the M-16s and asked me if I thought they might be hidden at Jack's girlfriend's house in Charlotte, North Carolina. I said, "What girlfriend?" The room was silent. They thought I knew. Maybe they thought that had been my motivation for turning him in. All those times he said he was going on some Special Forces mission out of town, he was actually living between our place and hers. I couldn't help but wonder if she knew about me. I also wondered if she knew he was a criminal. I shouldn't have been surprised, but to find out he had a steady relationship with someone else and to find out in a room full of Federal agents floored me. But that was the least of my worries. What I found out next changed everything. I went from being a scared, reluctant informant to being an angry, determined new person.

They discovered another storage locker, one I didn't know about. This was the biggie. Forget the collection of weapons I had seen—this was the real stash. Jack had in his possession: machine guns, anti-tank weapons, Claymore mines, TNT, plastic explosives, detonators, thousands of rounds of ammunition, grenades, anti-government fliers, as well as Nazi and white supremacy literature. This was much bigger than a couple of M-16s. Then they discovered he not only had a couple of local storage lockers, but many spread out across the Southern states. All of them were packed with weapons and ammunition. He even stooped so low as to store explosives under his parents' bed in Florida, without them even knowing it. It turns out that Jack was a big part of a weapons ring between South Carolina and other states and countries. Agents had been looking for him for a long time; they just didn't know who they were looking for.

To help me realize the true severity of my situation, the agents pulled out a file. They started talking about my accident, the one that totaled my car. Why would they be talking about the time when a drunk driver ran me off of the road? I was completely confused. They informed me that the driver was not only sober, but he was a member of Jack's Special Forces team. Apparently, a truck driver witnessed the incident, called in the license plate of the car, and it was traced to Jack's teammate. How could I not know this? How could they?

Suddenly, it all came back to me. The day of the accident. I was going to drive from South Carolina to Alabama to visit my parents. Jack was on his way out of town the same day for one of his supposed missions. I thought it was strange that he was so involved in helping me plan my trip, but I mistook his involvement for concern. He knew the minute I'd be leaving and exactly what route I'd be taking. He'd even insisted that I take a different route than the one I had planned. It was quicker, he assured me. I felt a chill when I also remembered him saying, "Trust me." Then I remembered his reaction to my news that I'd had an accident. It wasn't what I had expected from him at all. When he came home from his trip and saw me, he looked like he'd seen a ghost. I said I had some bad news, and he calmly said, "Okay." I told him the car was totaled, and still he just said, "Okay." I remembered it was a strange reaction, but then Jack was a strange man. When I lost our mailbox key, I thought he was going to kill me, but when I totaled the car, he just said, "Okay."

The agents assured me that it was no accident. Jack's teammate had tried to hurt me, maybe even kill me. Then I remembered the snorkeling incident in Panama. Was Jack trying to drown me, but then chickened out? Was he afraid he couldn't cover that one up? My God.

At least I would be safe now.

Journal entry, 22 February 1991

I told the agents about the divorce hearing and how we were both supposed to be present in Florida. They assured me they would wait until after the divorce to arrest him. Talk about scary. I had to face him one more time. Could I keep my composure and not let on that I had turned him in?

CHAPTER EIGHTEEN

I decided to move into a military hotel for the remainder of my time at Ft. Jackson. I didn't want my friends to be involved with me anymore than they had already been. I felt like a storm was coming, and I should be gathering supplies or something. I felt very alone.

I told the FBI and CID agents where I planned to stay, and they said they would see if they could arrange something better for me. The four agents left the room, and a few minutes later, one of them returned. He handed me his FBI business card, which had an address and phone number handwritten on the back. He said, "This is my house, but I'm in the process of moving out. You can stay there as long as you need to. Meet me there at 5 p.m., and I'll get you settled in." I naively assumed this was the place the four agents had agreed upon, so I felt safer already.

I arrived at the address on the card at 5 p.m. sharp. I rang the doorbell and the familiar agent answered. He closed and locked the door behind me. He said something strange like, "You're not wearing a wire are you?" I was uncertain of what he meant. As I stood there trying to figure out what I would be doing wearing a wire, he apologized and invited me to sit. If I had been in a clearer state of mind, this would have been a red flag, but I was living in a daze of fear, shock, and confusion since the moment I turned Jack in. At the most, I figured he just had a weird sense of humor. I noticed a smell coming from the kitchen, and the agent informed me that he was making dinner. He read my expression and said, "Don't worry; I'll be out of here in a while. I just thought we could share a nice dinner before I leave you to yourself. I figured you could use a good meal after all you've been through today." I realized I was being paranoid and forced myself to relax. After all, if you can't trust the FBI agent who is placed in charge of protecting you, who can you trust?

The agent said that dinner would take a while, so I was welcome to freshen up if I wanted. He showed me to my room and gave me clean towels. I decided to take a shower and rest until dinner. Things were going to be okay. After dinner, *the agent and I talked for a long while. I noticed photographs of what appeared to be his wife and kids. I thought maybe they had gone on ahead of him to wherever he was moving. I knew military families did that sometimes, so I could imagine that FBI families made similar moves. I asked him about his family, and he appeared very evasive of my questions. I started to wonder when he was leaving. I think he sensed my rising discomfort. He stood as if he was going to leave, and I stood to thank him for his hospitality. Then he started saying strange things and asking if I was wearing a wire again. This time I got scared and said maybe I should be the one to go. That's when his whole demeanor changed. He got ugly. He got dirty.*

I started to cry.

He said, "Don't cry," and then he put his arms around me. He tried to kiss me, and I pushed him away. He said, "I know you like it; you really enjoy being sexy, don't you? You can be a really sexy lady when you want to be." I thought he was a crazy man, mistaking me for someone else. He said, "Yeah, we had a great time looking at those sexy pictures of you." At first, I had no idea what he was talking about, but then it hit me like a Mack truck. A couple of years ago, Jack talked me into posing for some pictures for him. He kept them in a little album in his duffel bag and took them on trips with him. He swore that no one else would ever see them, so I obliged. After all, they were for my husband. Obviously, the pictures were in the storage locker that I hadn't known about, and the FBI agents helped themselves. At least one of them, that is. And this asshole assumed that if I would pose nude for photos for my husband, that I would jump at the chance to have sex with him.

He kept trying to kiss me and grope me, but I just kept pushing him away. I had to get out of there. This wasn't going to happen to me again. No way. He was between me and the door. He was a large man. This wasn't happening. An FBI agent would not be taking advantage of a young woman who was going through what I was. He knew I was afraid for my life. He knew I had no place to hide. I learned you can't trust anyone.

He had a gun.

I don't know where it came from; everything was happening so fast. He told me to get down on my knees. This wasn't the first time I'd had a gun pointed at my head; Jack used to do it for fun, but it's something you never get used to. I realized I'd be perfectly happy if I never saw another gun as long as I lived. On my knees, with tears streaming down my face, I awaited my next command. I was back there. I was back in that mode again. While holding the gun to my head with one hand, he grabbed a handful of my long hair with his other. Then he wrapped my hair around in his fist until his knuckles dug into my scalp. The cold steel of the gun barrel on the other side of my forehead felt surprisingly better than his filthy knuckles touching me. He forced me to give him a blow job at gunpoint, all the while telling me what a slut I was and no wonder Jack had cheated on me with that girl in Charlotte.

Allen realizes his hands are shaking. All he can say is, "My God."

I was lower than low. I had a scary suspicion that all hope was gone for me. I didn't think this guy was going to kill me once he'd gotten his way, but I thought my life was going to be worse than death. Just an endless, miserable existence, waiting for the next vulture to pick my bones dry.

The next morning, I woke up in a hotel. I couldn't remember how I had gotten out of the asshole's house, much less how I had found this place. It didn't matter. I realized I was going to be spending a lot of my life alone from now on. And I was okay with that thought. If you're alone, no one can hurt you.

CHAPTER NINETEEN

Journal entry, 1 March 1991

    I realized I would have to stay in touch with the authorities, so I took my chances and let one agent know how to reach me. One night I got a call from him, the FBI agent in charge of the case. He informed me that they had just arrested Jack in Panama. I asked about the divorce hearing, and he just said, "Sorry." I almost dropped the phone. Since I had only been staying at Ft. Jackson long enough to go to the divorce hearing in Florida, I told the agent I would be leaving the next day for California. He told me not to go just yet, that maybe he could help me with the divorce. The next day, he told me they had decided they would escort Jack to the hearing themselves. As scary as it sounded, having to face him like that, I was relieved to know it would soon be over. Two days before the court date, the agent informed me that they had "messed up." They couldn't even have Jack back from Panama in time for the divorce hearing, much less in Florida. I had been spending money on a hotel at Ft. Jackson, when I could have been halfway to California by then. I had also spent four hundred dollars on a plane ticket to Florida. That would have paid for a lot of gas. One CID agent said all they could do was give me a letter to give to the airline, in hopes of getting a refund for the ticket. I was almost out the door when something inside of me said, Wait a minute. Without me, they never would have solved that case, and I wasn't going to leave until they made a little more of an effort to help me. I knew there had to be something else they could do. I asked if they would call the courthouse in Florida and see if they would make an exception. The first phone call got us a stock reply from some receptionist saying, "No exceptions." Then the CID agent called the FBI and got them involved. They were able to speak to a judge, but not the one appointed to my case. The judge told them to send me anyway, but he couldn't make any promises. So here I was, flying to Florida, renting a car, getting a hotel, and sitting around, waiting to see a judge who may be telling me, "Tough luck." I had no idea if I would be leaving Florida a divorced woman or the wife of a convict.

SIDNEY

I left the courthouse, glad to be free of him. . .

Journal entry, 8 March 1991

My parents had no idea how bad things were; they only knew I was leaving my husband. Though worried, they were supportive of my decision and agreed that spending time with my sister would be a good thing. They loaned me what little money they had, which was just enough to buy a used Toyota Corolla. It took me all the way to California without a hitch.

Things were going to be okay.

CHAPTER TWENTY

Journal entry, 15 March 1991

I started looking for a job right away. The want ads in Los Angeles are sure different from the ones in South Carolina. There were ads for extras in movies, and all kinds of ads for dancers. "...no dancing experience necessary, partial nudity..." Not a chance! I went to the local Recruiter Station to let them know I had arrived. My unit in South Carolina was supposed to find me a reserve unit in California, but the recruiter informed me that most of the units in that area had been deployed to Saudi Arabia. Even if I did find a reserve unit, there wouldn't be much for me to do. What he said next hung in the air for a minute and made me feel like a fool. He said, "Why don't you go on active duty?" Now why hadn't I thought of that? It's what I had wanted right from the beginning; Jack was the reason I wasn't already on active duty, so what was stopping me now? Despite the warrant officer/doctor guy who had insisted I'd be in a wheelchair forever, I had recovered pretty well. Well enough to do a non-airborne job in the Army, I thought. If not, I would fake it. After all, I was tough now.

I got a call from one of the main CID agents on the case. He said Jack had escaped. My knees buckled under me and I had to grab onto a chair to keep from falling. Then he said not to worry because they quickly caught him, trying to fly back to the States. Deep breath. Apparently they arrested nine other people and were still gathering evidence for the upcoming trial.

Journal entry, 22 March 1991

I took all of the tests and physicals required for joining the Regular Army; surprisingly, I passed, and they wanted me to choose a job. The jobs available at the time were less than desirable, so I decided to keep checking back until they had something better to offer. The old me would have let them coerce me into taking the first job available, but the newly developing me decided it was about time I started thinking about what was best for me and for my future.

I got another call from the CID agent. They found the M-16s. They brought Jack's buddy Dale back from Saudi Arabia, where he was stationed at the time, and arrested him. The agent said, "Don't worry; he and Jack are going to be put away for a long time."

A few days later I was back at the MEPS (Military Entrance Processing Station), looking at the new jobs available. I called my sister to update her on what I'd found, and she said I missed an urgent call from the CID agent. So I called him from there. He said that Dale had escaped and that a lot of information had been printed about me in the local newspaper at Ft. Jackson. I thought, Wasn't anybody watching these guys? I guess they underestimated their evasive skills and determination. Since Dale was the one who was supposed to kill me if they ever got turned in, there was more than a little concern about where he was headed. The CID agent said that I could probably be put into the Witness Protection Program. I asked him if I could still be in the Army if I was, but he didn't think so. He said the military is a small world, and everybody knows someone from everywhere. I understood what he was trying to say.

They caught Dale on his way to California. . .

Journal entry, 29 March 1991

I found out more about the Witness Program than I'd ever wanted to. First of all, it's really called the Witness Security Program, or WITSEC for short. It's not exactly like what you see in the movies. I guess that's a good thing; they can't give all their secrets away. Also, it's not a case of all-or-nothing as far as the services they provide. A witness can be at one end of the spectrum and receive complete assistance in relocation, with no free contact with their family or friends, or they could become like me. I opted for the "I'll take care of myself and struggle every inch of the way" approach. Stupid girl.

If you've never heard these words from someone and had them really mean it, then you won't understand, but when the agent on the phone said, "How soon can you be out of there?" I had the feeling my life would never be the same.

Journal entry, 5 April 1991

I was very interested in doing some kind of Intelligence job in the Army, but that would have to wait. My recruiter, who was in on everything by now, took me straight to the social security office, where I applied for a new number. On the way there, we discussed possible new names for my new life. Was this really happening? It didn't completely register until weeks later, but I was building myself a new identity that day. It felt like I was a character in some movie. This certainly wasn't happening to me. Sheltered, boring, little old me. My recruiter was very sympathetic and helped me choose who I was to become for the rest of my life. He tried to lighten the situation by suggesting silly names or names whose initials spelled funny, three-letter words. I appreciated the gesture, but it was hard to laugh. Despite his teasing, I could see in his eyes that he was genuinely worried about me. He was not much older than me, and newly married. I think he was trying to imagine his wife going through this sort of thing. I told him I'd always envied other children when I was growing up who had names that allowed them to have nicknames. I also liked girls' names that sounded like boys' names, like Alex or Andie. He helped me decide on Sidney, A.K.A. Sid.

Allen can't believe he hasn't thought of this until just now... "So Sid wasn't her real name?" He remembers the name being scratched out on the inside cover of my journal. Still, he can't quite absorb this idea yet. It's just so hard to believe.

Journal entry, 12 April 1991

My trip to the social security office was to become the first of many trips to official offices, where I was to be treated like one of the following: an inconvenience, a fragile baby bird, a criminal, or a sideshow freak. No one ever knows quite how to handle me and my "situation." With my recruiter and me in the boss's office, and after a couple of phone calls to the CID and FBI, I had my new identity. So as not to link my old and new names and social security numbers in the computer in any way, they made it look like the old me had died, and the new me was a first-time applicant. New name chosen, new social security number, new Army-girl job in the works. I would soon go to the courthouse to make the name change legal. Everything was still going to be okay.

CHAPTER TWENTY-ONE

Journal entry, 19 April 1991

My recruiter and I returned to the MEPS, where I was to be interviewed for a secret clearance, which was necessary for a military intelligence job. The interviewer had to be made aware of my name and social security number changes, which didn't seem to matter to him. Good. They were on my side. He asked me a bunch of questions and then said the process would be complete after he interviewed everyone else for my case. No problem. He said he had to talk to my family, friends, neighbors, teachers. And my ex-husband. I almost laughed. I reminded him that Jack was in jail, and surely they must be able to make an exception in this case. He said, very smugly I might add, that they definitely had to interview him. So much for being on my side. He said they would have to tell Jack that I was applying for a secret clearance for a military intelligence job, and they would also have to tell him my new name. I couldn't believe what I was hearing. This was ridiculous. I guess having a new identity gives you the courage to say things that the old you never would have said because I stood up and said, "Why don't you just put me in the jail cell with him and hand him a gun?" I think I lost some points on the "ability to stay calm in stressful situations" category of my interview, but the bottom line was, I couldn't have a military intelligence job because of Jack. He's in jail and still ruining my life. I chose a job in the medical field. My military contract looked like someone else's. I had to remind myself it was mine.

Allen isn't surprised now when he realizes he's never actually *seen* my high school diploma, Associate's Degree, or anything else that might have a name on it.

Journal entry, 26 April 1991

I obviously couldn't stay with my sister anymore. She had enough trouble, worrying sick about me. I sure didn't want anyone shooting at her and her fam-

ily. I guess I should have been more afraid for myself than I was, but I was on auto pilot, in a state of disbelief, suspended above myself, or whoever that was who was taking over my body.

I wasn't due to ship out for my medical training for a couple of months. What was I going to do? I reluctantly called a friend of mine who was stationed in San Diego. I had met him on a military trip to Puerto Rico when I was in my reserve unit at Ft. Jackson and he was in the 82nd Airborne Division. Our scheduled parachute jumps got cancelled, so a group of us decided to share the cost of a rental car and tour the island of Puerto Rico. Patrick was part of that group. We all became friends and continued to keep in touch after the trip was over. Patrick had been sent to San Diego on recruiter duty, against his will. What guy from the 82nd Airborne Division wants to sit behind a desk and fill quotas every day? But I guess we all have to do our time. I decided to give him a call. What was I to say to him? How do you explain something like this to a distant friend, and then ask to stay at his house for a couple of months? I swallowed what was left of my humility and just asked. Thankfully, he said yes.

So here I was, hiding out in San Diego, just waiting to ship out to my new training station. I felt like I shouldn't get a job until all of my paperwork and identification was in my new name. Take no chances. The paranoia began to set in. I started to see my future clearly, realistically. I was scared.

My time with Patrick was surreal, but good. He treated me with respect. He treated me like a lady, something I had never experienced before. Most importantly, he expected nothing of me. He taught me that respect and kindness isn't too much to ask for. He gave me confidence and taught me that I didn't have to be treated badly by men.

I spent my time there trying to get used to my new name. In some ways, it felt good having a new name; it was like a shield or a veil I could hide behind. In other ways, it felt weird. Not just for the obvious reason, having people refer to you as some other name and remembering to respond to them quickly so as not to raise suspicion. But changing your name for a reason which is out of your control brings up all sorts of new thoughts and emotions. You think about that moment when you were born, and your proud parents had that perfect name *all picked out just for you. How heartbreaking it would be for them to know that their baby girl would someday have to abandon that name in order to save her own life. And speaking of abandonment, your mind starts to mess with you about this whole name change thing. You start thinking you need to abandon parts of your personality as well. You start thinking things like, "That was how I was in my old life. I need to be different now. If I look and even act like the same person, then someone might recognize me. Or more accurately, I might give myself away." Unfortunately, when you practice not giving yourself away, you become in danger of losing the real you.*

UNKNOWN AUTHOR

CHAPTER TWENTY-TWO

Journal entry, 3 May 1991

I'm pretty nervous about having to testify. They say that I'll have to inter-rupt my training to fly to South Carolina and maybe even Florida. How am I going to do this?

Journal entry, 14 June 1991

I'm two weeks into my training now, and they've informed me that Dale's wife has been stabbed to death. Well, half of their deal is done. I'm the only other missing link. I've been trying to convince myself that Dale and Jack would never actually kill someone, that it was all talk just to scare me. But I took away what was most precious to them. Their military careers and their weapons. I keep thinking it's me who ruined their lives, but that's not true. I have to remember that they did this to themselves. And they did this to me. Sure, no one made me turn them in, but if I hadn't, then where would we be? They would still be hoarding God knows how many weapons in endless storage lockers, just waiting to take over the government. And I would be a battered wife, a knowing ac-complice, and maybe even dead.

It's near impossible to concentrate on my studies. How am I supposed to pretend that everything is normal? I can't talk to anyone; I can't sleep. A lot has changed. The agents say I don't have to testify in court after all. Thank God. I don't think I could face him again. They said my written testimony would be enough. Jack has pleaded guilty to four of his thirteen counts. They gave him a plea bargain because he turned in a bunch of other people. So much for honor among thieves. They say he may not end up doing as much time as they had first envisioned. I have to wonder what that means.

Journal entry, 26 November 1991

And now they are putting me out of the Army. The only thing I ever wanted to do is be a soldier, and they're taking that away from me. Why? Be-cause I'm a walking target.

I thought things were going to be okay once I got settled into my new job, but I guess I was wrong. There I was two days ago, doing my job at the hospital, when two men and a woman came in wearing dark business suits. I thought to myself, "No." They were there for me, all right, and they were all FBI agents. They escorted me out of the hospital, which was extremely embarrassing because it appeared to my fellow soldiers that I was some kind of criminal. And I'll never be able to tell them anything different.

Once again, they are offering me full protection in the WITSEC Program. Wasting no time on tact, they told me that people were found in the area that were in Jack's group, and if they decided to blow up the barracks to get to me, my fellow soldiers would be in danger. I'm stationed at a prestigious military post, and they're telling me they don't want any bad publicity here. It's times like this that make you realize how insignificant you are as an individual human being in the big scheme of things.

I've often asked myself, if I knew then what I know now about how much I'd have to go through, would I still have turned him in? The answer is always—yes.

Still, no one can truly understand what I'm going through. They could never even imagine. I wouldn't believe it if I wasn't going through it myself. Maybe someday I'll have a normal life. . .

Allen is thinking about my broken pelvis from airborne school and how that had seemed like a perfectly reasonable explanation for leaving the military. He had wondered, though, why I hadn't gone back on active duty after I healed. He knew I'd loved the Army life. What he hadn't known was that I had more than one reason for not going back into the military.

The Veteran's Administration, who took over my medical care after my discharge, considered me legally disabled. Physically and mentally. Of course, the damage to my pelvis and reproductive organs was obvious. But the other, the mental part. . . That's a lot harder to explain or to even understand myself.

They call it Posttraumatic Stress Disorder (PTSD). That's a fancy way of saying fucked-up. It hits you out of nowhere and when you least expect it. I could be sitting there at a restaurant, perfectly fine, and suddenly I would see someone. Someone who looked familiar. Too familiar. Before I could take the time to construct in my brain whether or not this person was a good guy or a bad guy, I would be in a state of panic. And the nightmares. Too many to count. The same old dream, every time. They found me and were chasing me. Sometimes the scenery would change, but the outcome was always the same. They killed me every time. I would wake up shaking and sweating, sometimes with bruises and scratches on my arms. I used to call it "fighting the bad guys in my sleep."

Unfortunately, there's no support group for someone like me. There are PTSD support groups at the VA, good ones, I hear. But they consist mostly of Vietnam veterans. I don't think I would fit into that group. And it's not like I could just get together with other people in my situation. How do you start a support group for federal witnesses? It's not like you can just look them up or put up fliers, inviting them to the local coffee shop. I wonder how many of us there are out there.

I had become very good at hiding the physical pain of my disabled body from friends, the Army, and even from Allen. I was able to fool nearly anyone into thinking I was okay. But even if I had been okay, I couldn't have gone back in if I'd wanted to. As stubborn as I am, I actually tried. I thought I could fool the Army into thinking I had healed. I didn't even get past the recruiter. As he was looking over my DD-214, or military discharge form, he began to laugh. I asked him what was so funny, and he said, "Boy, this is quite a typo." He pointed to the number four which was occupying the box entitled "RE code." Still not seeing the humor in a number in a box, I asked him to explain. He said, "RE stands for your re-entry code. They assign you a code, telling recruiters what status you were when you got discharged. That code also tells us whether or not you can go back into the military. A one can get back in, no problem. A two means you were injured, but can get back in with a waiver if you're healed. A three means you committed a crime and can't go back in at all." He hesitated. I couldn't wait. "And a four?" He chuckled. "A four means you're retired...or dead!" Even though he was reaching for the phone to call whoever, to ask about the "typo," I already knew the outcome. Not only had they put me out of the Army, they made damn sure I couldn't go back in. They'd thought of everything. The voice on the other end of the line apparently asked the recruiter to read what was typed in another little box. Who would have thought such a little box could have such a big impact on someone's whole future? He answered, "By order of the Secretary of the Army." That was it. Silence. Silence while the voice explained something lengthy to the recruiter sitting in front of me. The disappointed and bewildered recruiter hung up and gave me a suspicious stare. He explained that when a soldier has a re-entry code of a four, and under "reason" it says "By order of the Secretary of the Army," that it means the soldier's files are Top Secret, and the code can only be changed by the secretary himself.

The recruiter's curiosity was obvious, and he asked me if I knew why this was the case with my files. My instincts told me to play dumb. My newly developing sarcastic side wanted to say, "I could tell you, but I'd have to kill you." But none of it mattered. I simply stood up, thanked him for his time, and left, realizing my dream of having a military career was over.

CHAPTER TWENTY-THREE

Allen just can't stop wondering what all I must have given up. How different would my life have been if I'd been able to live it freely, without fear?

Little does Allen know, I almost quit school altogether. As a matter of fact, I almost quit before I even got started. Because of the rush of my FBI-assisted discharge from the Army, there was a problem with my paperwork. In order for them to give me an honorable discharge, they had to say I got out *voluntarily*. Little did I know at the time, that if you get out voluntarily before your contract is up, you forfeit all of your benefits. Even the ones you paid for. Although I had paid every payment into my GI Bill College Fund, I lost everything that day. After the whirlwind of being a witness and relocating had subsided, I decided to go back to school. It was then that I found out I had lost my benefits. I fought the VA for nine long years before finally winning my benefits back. After all, I earned them, even paid for them, so why should I give them up without a fight?

Feeling a renewed sense of hope, I walked into the admissions office of the university with paperwork in hand. Because I'd had a name *and* social security number change, I knew I needed to prove to someone in charge that my Associate's Degree (that I'd finally finished after leaving Jack) and other transcripts were actually mine. I was prepared. Or so I thought. Nothing could have prepared me for what was about to happen. The lady in charge of admissions listened to my story, looked at my various documents and photo IDs, and then called campus security. I was appalled. At first, I thought she was assuming I was a fraud, and she was turning me in to be arrested. To the officer on the other end of the line, she said, "I'm afraid we have a potentially dangerous situation here." Was she calling *me* dangerous? But when she hung up the phone, she clarified. She told me, "The last thing the university wants is another Columbine." She thought that having me around would put my fellow students in danger. The university couldn't afford any bad publicity. This was sounding all too familiar. A walking target. That's what the Army had considered me, and I guess the label was going to stick. Why? Because I did the right thing. I turned in the bad guys, and now I was being treated like the criminal.

After months of being ignored by the admissions staff, I'd had enough. I hadn't come this far to be turned away unfairly. After hearing a news story about felons being given a second chance and being given full-ride scholarships to universities, I grabbed my car keys. Why should felons be given second chances at a normal life, while the ones who put them behind bars continued to be punished? I drove straight to the university, marched into the admissions office, and handed the Columbine lady the same stack of paperwork from months earlier. I said, "My lawyer says you have to at least accept my application, and then you have to have a legally valid reason for rejecting me." She looked disgusted, but took my paperwork. Three days later, I received my letter of acceptance.

Unfortunately, this was only the beginning of my struggles while in college. My airborne school accident had left me permanently disabled, and carrying loads of books across a large campus kept me from avoiding this reality any longer. I was forced to start using my handicapped hang tag so I could park closer to my classes. Because I didn't *look* disabled, my fellow students assumed I must be borrowing someone else's hang tag just to get prime parking spaces. Instead of doing the logical, mature thing and asking me about my disability, they took it upon themselves to harass me. They left nasty notes on my car, scratched my car several times, and even got campus parking services in on the harassment. They told parking services that I was using someone else's hang tag, and instead of asking me for proof, they just started ticketing me. Even after I offered proof, I kept coming out of class just to find a new parking ticket on my windshield day after day. Unbelievable. As if I didn't have enough to worry about. It was beginning to feel like the whole world was against me. What had I done to deserve this cruelty? All I wanted was a normal life.

If it hadn't been for Gary, who was our instructor, my advisor, and protector, I don't think I would have made it to graduation. He encouraged me to put the emotions I was experiencing into my art. He reminded me that I was still the same girl inside, and that nothing and no one could take that away. That's why it was especially touching when at graduation, just before receiving my Bachelor's Degree, he leaned down and whispered, "Congratulations, Melinda." It had been so long since I'd heard my real name, that it felt good just hearing him say it.

Allen is putting my journal back in its place on the desk. He's sitting there for a minute, not sure if his legs will support him yet. He has that feeling you have the day after you've seen a particularly incredible movie, the kind that leaves you finding deeper meaning in the plot the more you look back on it. He understands now that there was so much more to me; my plot was deeper than anyone will ever know.

CHAPTER TWENTY-FOUR

It's been three months now, and the fog is starting to lift from Allen's brain. He's beginning to see clearly again and even finds himself whistling on his way to the mailbox. His cell phone rings as he is unlocking box #12. He's balancing the phone between his shoulder and his cheek while he's removing the stack of mail. It's Mark. He hasn't heard from him since the day of my funeral. He's assuming Mark is checking up on his progress as the widowed husband, just like everyone else keeps doing, as he shifts through the letters and bills.

When are they going to stop sending my mail to Allen, for God's sake?

Mark is starting off with the normal small talk, as expected, and Allen is halfway listening as he tears open the letter from one of the big publishing companies. "Dear Sidney, we are pleased to inform you…blah, blah, blah…blah, blah, blah…will be published. Congratulations." He's feeling a pain in his heart he could never begin to describe. He's so proud of me. He almost forgets Mark is on the phone until he hears the word "sniper." He's snapping back into reality. He's asking Mark to repeat what he just said. Mark's telling him, "We've connected the sniper to an employee at one of the publishers Sid had submitted her book to. We *told* her not to do it, Allen. We *told* her it was too risky. Allen, they found her because of her book. I'm sorry. I thought you would want to know."

Allen is pressing the off button on his cell phone and locking the mailbox. On his walk back to the house, he's realizing that he will never get over me—his unknown author—Sid.

ABOUT THE AUTHOR

The author, who goes by the pen name Sidney, has created a suspenseful drama based on her true-life experiences. Through her work, she desires to see people become truly appreciative of their "normal" lives and to become a testimony to those in controlling or abusive situations.

"Sidney" was awarded the Army Achievement Medal for her contribution to the military and the U.S. Government. She has a Bachelor's Degree in Fine Art and is a working artist. She enjoys travel, true friends, reading and being outdoors.

Cover design is by the author